Plug-Horse Derby

EMMA L. BROCK

Plug-Horse Derby

NEW YORK ALFRED·A·KNOPF

L.C. catalog card number: 55–8947

© ALFRED A. KNOPF, INC., 1955

THIS IS A BORZOI BOOK,
PUBLISHED BY ALFRED A. KNOPF, INC.

CONTENTS

SOMETHING UNEXPECTED   1

AND THEN—   14

PLOW BOY   26

ON THE WAY   44

THE SECRET WORD   59

PLOW BOY'S CARRIAGE   71

THE PLUG-HORSE DERBY   90

WHO WINS?   107

Plug-Horse Derby

SOMETHING
UNEXPECTED

"When will something happen?" Nancy said to herself. "Whenever will it? Something unexpected. When?"

She pulled up her jeans and looked at the white socks that crowned her scuffed-off Oxfords. She needed clean ones. They were grimy with hay dust, but they rolled themselves down fashionably, Nancy thought. Her mother said they were foolish things to wear around a farm, but nevertheless she cheerfully churned a dozen or more of them in the washer every Monday.

"Let white socks be white socks," Nancy's mother always said.

Nancy sat on the back steps of the farmhouse and stared at her off-white socks.

"Something unexpected. Something more exciting than anything that has ever happened to me before. A letter, maybe," Nancy said. "An unexpected letter from—from an unexpected person with some unexpected and exciting news!"

Or an unexpected ringing of the telephone. Or a present, an unexpected present.

"Oh, yes," Nancy thought. "That's it, a present!"

A present all knobbly and tied with string. Lumps here and there. Exciting bumps that hid secret wonderments. What would be in it?

"Oh, something," Nancy said. "Something wonderful that I don't even know I'm wanting. Oh, yes!"

She rocked her heels back and forth on the gravel walk. The pebbles gritted a gritty rhythm.

"You could run down to the box," her mother called, "and get the mail. Will you, Nancy? Dinner'll be ready by the time you come back."

The warm spicy smell of her mother's stew drifted out from the kitchen.

"Mmm," said Nancy. "I'll hurry, but there won't be a thing there."

Nancy put her fingers between her lips and whistled so

[2]

shrilly that she jumped at the sound of it. The black horse over in the grassy plot beyond the barn looked up at the sound. The last green mouthful was still limply hanging from his lips.

"Come on, Plow Boy, we're going for the mail."

Plow Boy plodded obediently toward her, chewing at the mouthful as he came. He neatly pulled in the tag-ends of grass. Nancy climbed the pasture fence and threw her skinny legs over the horse's broad back. She looked very small on the black bulk of him.

"Gid-ap!" And she slapped him on the rump. "Just maybe the letter might be there. Gid-ap!"

Plow Boy lifted his head and trotted between the clover field and the pasture lot toward the highway. In half a minute they came to the mail box on its tip-tilted post. It had REED in black stenciled letters on the side.

Would *the* letter be there today? Nancy jerked down the door and snatched out the mail. The horse shifted his feet and began ambling toward the pasture grass. Nancy shuffled over the pieces of mail. An ad about tractors, an ad about weed-killers, a letter in Aunt Martha's comfortable writing. A bill from the feed man, a check from the milk firm, a farm journal, her mother's magazine. Nancy riffled through the pages and shook it. No letter fell out. Nothing!

"Bother!" said Nancy.

[4]

The unexpected letter from the unexpected person was not there!

"It never comes! Never!"

She urged Plow Boy back to the mail box and peered in again to make sure. Empty! She slammed the door. She stuffed the letters down the neck of her sweater and jammed the magazines under her arm.

"Never!"

She pulled the morning paper from the yellow cylinder with *Pioneer Express* on the side. She flipped over the paper and looked at the back page. What was happening to Ella Cinders today? Nothing much ever happened. It always seemed as if it would happen and it never did. It was too slow. She wanted things to happen fast and big and *soon*, Nancy did. It could not be too soon!

She poked the paper under her other arm and pushed her hands into the pockets of her jeans.

"Home, Plow Boy. It's stupid. Life is stupid and it's stew for dinner."

But the dinner was good. The dinners were always good and so were the suppers and breakfasts. Nothing unexpected ever happened. Nothing ever scorched, the cakes never fell, the milk never soured. Everything was always good. It was dull.

Nothing different ever happened. Her father was read-

[5]

ing the paper as he always did. Her brother Bill was asking for a third helping before he had finished chewing the last of the second, as he always did. And Jens, the man who helped her father with the farm work, was reading every word of the ads as he always did. Her mother was throwing eager glances at her magazine on the corner of the table just the way she did every time it came. Nancy gulped down her milk.

"As I always do," she thought. "Every day, and every meal, and every year, one after another. Milk after milk after milk!"

Her father laughed suddenly.

"That'll be amusing," he said.

He always was thinking things in the paper were funny that were not funny at all. Nancy looked at him impatiently from under her eyebrows. What was it now?

"A plug-horse derby! That's a laugh."

"A what?" asked Bill, holding a fork very full of stew half-way to his mouth.

Nancy glared at him. He looked just silly, sitting there with his mouth standing open as he had opened it to put in the stew. His eyes were like blue ponds in his brown face. They did not even wink. He looked ridiculous. He was an oaf!

"A plug-horse derby, a race for farm horses at the State

[6]

Fair. This is what it says: 'Farmers in this state will have a chance to win $750 in prizes in a Plug-Horse Derby, a new event at the State Fair this year. The unglamorous work-horse,'" he went on, "'will race a quarter-mile track on the Fair grounds on Labor Day afternoon, September 1st.

"'The winner of the contest, which is restricted to work- or draft-horses, will receive a prize of $250, second place $100, and the next eight places $50 each. Only horses weighing 1300 pounds or more, owned by residents of this state will be eligible.'"

Nancy was staring with her blue eyes fast on her father's face. She was not only holding a forkful of stew half-way to

[7]

her mouth, she was dribbling it off the fork. And it was dribbling not only on her plate, but also on the table-cloth.

"Take care, Nancy," her mother said. "Please pay attention." Nancy dropped her fork back on her plate.

" 'Entries,' " her father continued, " 'which will close on August 10th, must be made on official entry blanks which are now appearing in the *Pioneer Express* along with complete rules.

" 'Preliminary races will be run at the State Fair track August 22nd. The ten winners in the preliminaries will compete in the official Plug-Horse Derby on Labor Day.' "

"Let's see the entry blank," said Nancy.

"It must be on another page," said her father.

Nancy had abandoned her stew altogether and was leaning over her father's shoulder as he leafed through the paper.

"There," she said.

In large black type was the ad, with a rather chunky looking farm horse and a money-bag lumpy with dollar signs.

" 'Mr. Farmer,' " Nancy read. " 'One of your work-horses may win $250. Enter *Pioneer Express* Plug-Horse Derby, to be run in conjunction with the State Fair.'

[8]

Here's the entry blank. It says: 'I have read and agree to abide by all the rules of the *Pioneer Express* Plug-Horse Derby and wish to enter—so-many—horses in the race, each of which weighs 1300 pounds or more. Name, address.' "

"I'm entering Plow Boy right here and now," shouted Nancy. "Let's see the rules."

There were paragraphs and paragraphs of fine print. Nancy's face was close to her father's as they read them together.

"Here's one," Nancy's father said. " 'All horses must be at the scales located near the Administration Building at 9 A.M., Friday, August 22nd, for official weighing.' "

"Plow Boy's more than 1300 pounds," Nancy shouted. "Does it say anything about age? For me, I mean. Does it say you have to be more than eleven going on twelve?"

She and her father both looked carefully through the fine print from beginning to end.

"Nothing about age. No, nothing at all," said her father. "You can enter Plow Boy yourself because he is really your horse."

"Oh, sure, Dad. Where's your pen? I'll do it right now. Where's your pen, Mother?"

"My pen is on the desk in the living room," her mother said. "In the back corner on the right side. The right thing

[9]

in the right place, I always say. And then there you find it."

Nancy spread the paper on the kitchen table.

"Better print," her father said. "Not too heavy."

So Nancy printed in small tidy letters that exactly fitted the space: "Nancy Jane Reed, Windy Hill Farm, County Road E."

The pulpy newsprint paper made little fuzzes on all sides of the letters, but it was easy to read in spite of them. Nancy looked at it proudly as she carefully cut it out with the kitchen shears.

"I'm entered," she said. "Now an envelope and I'll mail it right away."

[10]

"No hurry," Bill scoffed. " 'Twon't go until tomorrow anyway."

He had finished his third helping of stew and two helpings of tapioca pudding. He was slouched back in his chair and was looking sourer than a sour green apple. His eyes were more like thunder clouds than blue pools.

"A girl can't ride," he said. "No girl could win a race."

"Wait and see," Nancy said. "You wait and see."

"Whoever heard of a girl jockey?" growled Bill. "Whoever heard of a girl jockey at the Kentucky Derby? Humph, Jens? Ever see a girl jockey at the Kentucky Derby?"

"Well, no," Jens said, "but—"

"But I'll win," said Nancy.

"How about the dishes, Nancy?" her mother said. "Bill, you help carry them out. Plow Boy is a good horse and Nancy is a good rider. The best horse wins the race."

"Here's something we didn't pay attention to before," Nancy's father said.

"What?" cried Nancy in alarm. "Not—"

" 'Owners,' " read her father, " 'may enter as many horses as they wish.' "

"Oh," gasped Nancy. "But I can ride only one horse at a time."

"There's Pete. I could ride Pete," Bill said hopefully. "He's as good as Plow Boy. Even better."

[11]

"They're both good," said Bill's father. "Together they won the pulling contest at the County Fair. Remember?"

Bill was looking more cheerful now that he could ride in the derby too.

"I'll ride Pete and beat you to pieces, Nance."

"You'll see," Nancy answered. "You never have before."

Nancy was shaking soap flakes into the dish water. More soap, more soap until the froth piled up into crisp white horses. You could hear them crackling as they sped from cups to plates, to saucers. More soap, more horses. Galloping, galloping. The Plug-Horse Derby. Look at them go. One horse was leading them all. Plow Boy was leading them all. Nancy did a little jig as she watched them.

Jens was standing in the kitchen doorway. He always wore a grin, but the one he was wearing at that moment was really too wide for his face. His wood-shaving hair showed below his cap.

"Tell you what, Nancy," he said. "I'm going to the city tonight and I'll mail your letter for you."

"Oh, Jens," Nancy cried.

"It'll be picked up tonight and delivered early tomorrow morning."

"Oh, Jens! That will be just wonderful. It might be the first one to arrive. Oh, goody! Thanks, Jens."

[12]

"That's all right," Jens said. "It's nothing. I want to see you win."

The soap-suds foam was still rising. Yes, Plow Boy was ahead. As Nancy slopped the suds, he ran faster than ever.

It took Nancy 73½ minutes to wash the dishes that noon.

AND THEN—

Now that something unexpected and exciting had really happened, Nancy was no longer grumping and grumbling about. She was no longer plodding around at her share of the farm work on the Oxfords that took up so much room wherever they went.

"Yo ho," Nancy sang. "Yo ho, humpty, humpity, ho, ho!"

She was tripping around like a happy fairy. Of course the Oxfords still clumped. They were that kind and they were on the ends of Nancy's legs. Her legs were the clumping kind, too.

"Yo ho, humpty, humpity, ho, ho!"

"Is there anything sillier than a girl?" Bill growled as he

[14]

watched her. "How many yeast cakes did you eat? You're sure yeasty."

"I'm going to win the race, win the race!" Nancy sang.

"Oh, yeah?" said Bill. "You'll see."

The morning after the entry blank was sent in, Nancy rode Plow Boy out to the far fields to help shock the grain. Her father and Jens were there, and Bill, too. They had twenty-five acres of it and it was all ripe and ready. Her father had been cutting it and now the bundles must be stacked up in shocks to dry. Who knew when a thunderstorm or a big wind would come along and ruin it? So they worked as hard as they could all morning long.

When they returned to the house for dinner, they found Nancy's mother smiling widely to herself. She was usually a serious person and smiles meant something special.

"Whatever is it?" Nancy asked.

"There was a telephone call this morning," her mother said mysteriously.

"Who was it?" Nancy squealed.

That was one of the things she had been wanting to happen. An unexpected telephone call from an unexpected person.

"Who was it?" she asked.

"Someone who wanted to speak to Miss Nancy Jane Reed," her mother said.

[15]

"To me? How wonderful! Who was it? Who could want to speak to me?"

Her mother was still smiling.

"Who?" cried Nancy.

Her father and Bill and Jens were standing around, too, waiting for the answer.

"The reporter from the *Pioneer Express.*"

"And I wasn't here," Nancy moaned.

"Your entry blank was the first one in this morning and he called up at once."

"Oh, it was the first. Jens mailed it last night so it would be early. What did he want?"

"To interview you, he said. To find out about you and the horse and everything," her mother said.

"And did you tell him?"

"He wanted to talk with you, Nancy."

"Oh, dear," moaned Nancy. "I could have come in a minute on Plow Boy."

"If I had had any way to call you," her mother said.

"If this keeps up, we'll have to get one of those big bells that they used to have on farms to call the people to dinner." And Nancy's father laughed.

"But he is coming here tomorrow morning," her mother said.

[16]

"Oh!" Nancy sighed, clasping her hands.

"I took the liberty of making an appointment for him at eight o'clock. I told him you would be going out to work early."

"Did you tell him Plow Boy is going to win the race?"

"Now did you, Martha? Did you tell him we have the winning horse?" Nancy's father was laughing and winking at Bill.

"Yes, did you, Mom?" giggled Bill. Women were the silliest things.

Nancy's mother was looking very solemn. She did not realize that they were teasing her.

"Well now, I did just that," she said. "I said that horse is a fast horse and that girl is a fast rider and she's sure she'll win. So I'm sure she will, too. 'She could win a Kentucky Derby,' I said."

"Oh, Mom! You didn't!" shrieked Nancy.

They were all laughing. Nancy's mother looked from one to the other of them and smiled faintly.

"Was that so funny?" she asked.

"Boy, is it ever!" Nancy's father said.

"It's the truth and what's more I said something else."

"No! What? Tell!" they said in a chorus.

"Well, I said: 'That prize is coming to this family in any

case because if Plow Boy does not win, there's the other horse we are entering and he could win the race standing still.' "

"Mom!"

"Mom! You didn't!"

"Good for you, Martha!"

"Well now, dinner is ready. It's chicken and dumplings."

"You're sure a good advertiser, Martha," Nancy's father said, shouting with laughter.

"I was just telling the truth. Wait and see. How many dumplings to start with, Dad?"

The dumplings and most of the chicken had disappeared before they went back to the far field to do more shocking. Nancy was rather floating on a cloud because of the reporter. She floated all evening long and all night, too.

By the time the reporter came the next morning, Nancy, in a pair of clean socks and polished shoes, had rubbed Plow Boy down and combed his mane and tail.

"You must look your best for the newspaper man," she said. "And do try to keep from nibbling grass while he is interviewing you. It isn't a bit polite."

At exactly five minutes before eight the reporter drove into the yard, bringing with him a staff photographer. Nancy was breathless.

"Oh, are you planning to take his picture? Goody!"

She was glad she had groomed him up a bit.

"Where do you want him to pose?"

"We want you riding him," the photographer said.

"Oh, me too?" said Nancy. "I thought you would want just the winner."

"The jockey, too." The photographer grinned.

"Here, I'll give you a leg up," the reporter said.

"I can get on from the fence over there," said Nancy.

"Try this," said the reporter, holding his hands out for a step.

Nancy reached with her hands for Plow Boy's neck, put one large Oxford—she was glad she had polished it—on the reporter's hands and swung up to the horse's back.

"Thanks."

She was almost choking. It made her feel like a princess or a lady or something grand to be helped like that!

"Now," said the photographer, aiming his camera.

"Hold your head up, P.B.," Nancy ordered. "Please excuse him. He's the eatingest horse I ever knew."

Flash went the camera.

"Now, walk ahead slowly. We want him in action."

"Gid-ap," said Nancy, and Plow Boy lifted one foot after the other in the right order and thudded down the roadway.

[20]

The photographer ran backward in front of him, squinting and aiming the camera. Nancy hoped he would not fall down and break it—or his neck.

Flash went the camera.

"Another one, in case that isn't good."

Flash the camera went again.

"He has good nerves, that horse," the reporter said. "Never jumped once at the flashes."

"Oh, he isn't a bit skittish," Nancy said.

"You're going to win the race, your mother told me."

"I think we can," Nancy answered. "There were some riding horses that came along one day. And I raced the kids on them and we won. Plow Boy can beat any horse around here. He doesn't like any horse to get ahead of him. Not ever."

"That's what your mother told me, too."

"Oh, yes," said Nancy's mother very seriously. "He'll win. The best horse is sure to win."

The reporter slapped Plow Boy's neck and rubbed his nose.

"He likes you, Mr.—I don't know your name," said Nancy.

"Johnny," said the reporter. "Just call me Johnny, and this here's Steve."

"Hi, Steve," said Nancy. "There's just one thing I'm

[21]

really worried about," Nancy admitted. "Just one thing."

"What is that?" asked Johnny.

"If Plow Boy should see a bit of green grass, he'd leave the race and go and eat it."

"Now there is that danger, isn't there?" Johnny said to Nancy's mother.

"Yes, Plow Boy likes grass," she answered. "Good eating makes a fit horse."

"But, come to think of it, is there any grass near that track, Steve?"

"Is there ever!" Steve replied. "The whole arena in the center of the track is grassy."

"Too bad," said Johnny.

"Oh, well, we'll have to hope he won't want any right then," Nancy said. "There wouldn't be time to eat grass in the middle of a race. I'm sure of that."

"What are you planning to do with the money?" Johnny asked. "It's $250, you know. That's a lot of money."

"Is it ever!" said Steve.

"It's more than I ever dreamed of," Nancy said, letting herself slide down from the horse's back. "I really don't know how much it really is."

"It will buy a great many things," Nancy's mother said.

[22]

"I may start with a saddle," Nancy said. "Plow Boy wants a saddle to be more stylish. Those riding horses had nice saddles and so we want a saddle. Don't we, P.B.?"

"It'll buy more than a saddle," Johnny said.

"I'll have to think up something else. I've known about it only a day, you know."

"Sure," said Johnny. "Now tell me about yourself. How old are you? Where do you go to school? Have you always lived here?"

Nancy answered all those questions and many more while Johnny wrote the answers down in a plump note-book. It was fun being interviewed. She felt just like a movie star and she hoped that Johnny would ask for her autograph. But he did not. He closed the book and stuffed it into his pocket.

"O.K., Steve, let's push on. Thanks, Mrs. Reed and Nancy. See you at the races."

"Oh, thanks, Johnny. And thank you, Steve, for the pictures."

"O.K.! Don't let anything happen to the derby champion!" Johnny laughed.

"Oh, no. We won't," Nancy promised.

"O.K.," said Steve and Johnny and away they drove in their car.

[23]

Nancy watched them until the car turned onto the highway by the mail box.

"Well, I must get to work," she said, as if she were in the middle of a dream.

She led Plow Boy to the fence, climbed up on the fence and swung herself over his broad back. A saddle would be nice.

"Isn't it wonderful, Mom? Isn't it all wonderful? The photographer and the way Johnny helped me up on P.B.! What an adventure! What a wonderful adventure! Isn't it, Mom? At last something unexpected has happened!"

"Yes, Nancy," her mother answered. "It is wonderful, Nancy."

She watched Nancy riding gaily away to the far field on her race horse. Nancy was singing the song she had made.

"Yo, ho! Humpty, humpity, ho, ho!"

"What if she should not win," her mother was wondering. "What if she should not win."

[25]

PLOW BOY

"You ride like a girl," Bill said.

"And I am a girl, aren't I? What else?" snapped Nancy.

"No girl can win a race."

"You wait and see."

"You're too small for the horse, too. You look silly up there—and scared."

"I am not scared. How ridiculous! I've ridden Plow Boy for three years, ever since we got him. How could I be scared?"

"O.K., you're not scared," said Bill. "But you can't win the race. See?"

Nancy clucked to Plow Boy and galloped off along the road. Bill was an oaf.

[26]

They were exercising their horses on the quiet side road to Afton. There were very few cars there. Every evening they gave the horses a workout to prepare them for the races. Their father and Jens had been pouring all kinds of advice on them.

"Let them run until they want to stop, kids," their father said. "Don't push them too much at first."

"Yes, Dad."

"And make Plow Boy hold his head up," Jens said. "He looks beaten before he starts with it hanging that way. There was no horse like that at Churchill Downs."

"Sure, Jens," Nancy said. "It's a bad habit he has."

"He's no race horse," scoffed Bill. "Look how peppy Pete is."

"Watch it, Bill," said his father. "Neither one of them is a race horse. They're just ordinarily good farm horses."

"And remember," Jens said, nodding his head and looking very wise, "good training is the secret of success."

Jens knew a lot about horse racing. But then he had held some horses at the Kentucky Derby once, when he was a boy working near Churchill Downs. So of course he knew all about racing.

So now Nancy was "training" Plow Boy for the great Plug-Horse Derby on Labor Day. She would begin with his head.

"Plow Boy!" she said severely. "Plow Boy!"

The horse turned his ears in their sockets so that he could hear her better.

"Plow Boy!" she yelled. "Do you hear me? Hold up your head!"

And Plow Boy did. He was so startled by that fierce tone in Nancy's voice that he lifted his head and skipped a few steps in alarm.

"That's better," Nancy said. "Keep it up now," and she pulled on the reins to try to hold the head in place.

Plow Boy, being an intelligent horse, knew that pulling on the reins meant stop at once. So he stopped at once. And dropped his head.

"Oh, Plow Boy," Nancy groaned. "What am I going to do with you? You're hopeless, just hopeless!"

Plow Boy turned his ears toward the front again. Perhaps he did not wish to hear Nancy's scolding. He was really a very pleasant character. He was strong and kind. He did whatever Nancy told him to when he could understand what she wanted. And he could run and gallop as fast as fast.

Now she turned him toward home. She was clucking to him and slapping him in the ribs with her heels. It meant go. So Plow Boy went.

[28]

"Gid-ap!" and Nancy slapped him again. "Faster, P.B., faster! Oats, oats!"

When Plow Boy heard those words: "Oats, oats," he lifted his head and galloped faster than ever. His big feet thudded and thundered on the dirt road. Nancy was crouching down over him, holding fast to the reins.

"Oats!" she cried, and Plow Boy dashed past Bill and Pete leaving them in a brown dust cloud.

"Whoa, there, P.B.," Nancy called pulling on the reins. "Whoa! So that's the way to make him go. I'll just talk about oats during the race. That's just what I'll do!"

The horse trotted on eagerly until he reached the mail box and then the barn.

"Here you are," Nancy said. "Here's a few oats. You're too hot and tired to eat much right now."

Plow Boy munched noisily and happily at the oats while Nancy rubbed him down.

"The secret word!" Nancy said. "The princess whispered the secret word into the ear of her night-black steed and he fled over the mountain faster than the wind. 'Oats,' whispered the princess, 'Oats!' Oh, P.B., how ridiculous!"

Nancy was shouting with laughter when Bill came into the barn with his race horse Pete. Bill's pond-blue eyes had a surprised look in them.

"Gee!" he said. "That horse can go when he wants to."

[30]

Nancy smiled and she was surprised, too. It did not sound like Bill.

"I thought it was a thunderstorm passing right by me. Too bad he can't run like that all the time. Too bad he's just a plow horse. And you ought to learn to ride him. You were flapping like a loose sail!"

That sounded more like Bill.

"He just wanted to get home," Nancy said. "To eat."

"Whew," said Bill. "He wanted to eat bad, didn't he?"

"Sure," Nancy said, as she gave Plow Boy a last pat and went into the house.

The days of August were passing by. Nancy crossed them off on the calendar hanging in the kitchen. Every day or so an ad for the derby appeared in the paper with a new application blank. Every day over the radio the announcer said: "Farmers! Don't delay. Enter your horses in the Plug-Horse Derby. For rules and entry blank see the *Pioneer Express.* Hurry!"

"It's the tenth, isn't it, that the paper is going to let us know if our horses are to run in the race?" Nancy asked at breakfast one day.

"Yes," her father said. "They send out acceptances on the tenth."

"And on the eleventh the letters will come and be put in our mail box? Huh?"

"Just about," said her father.

"And do you know what day it is today?" Nancy continued. "The eleventh. Today is the eleventh and we get our letters from the paper today. As soon as I have fixed the chickens and weeded that flower garden, I'm going down to sit by the mail box."

"Ha, ha!" scoffed Bill.

"And I'll bring your letter right to you, Bill."

"You'd better," said Bill. "See that you do."

So when the postman drove along in his brown car, there was Nancy perched on the back of Plow Boy waiting for the mail.

"Why, hi there," called the postman.

"Hi, Mr. Janssen. Any mail today? Any special mail?"

"Well, I don't know about special mail, but there is a lot of it."

"Goody," cried Nancy and she pulled Plow Boy over to the mailman's car. Magazines, letters, bills, ads.

"What a lot," Nancy said. "Oh, here it is. 'Nancy Jane Reed' from the *Pioneer Express.* Wait and I'll let you know what it says. It's about the races."

Nancy tore the envelope to pieces trying to get the letter out.

"Yep. It's O.K. Plow Boy can race in the trial races. For the derby, you know. He's O.K."

[32]

"Well, congratulations," said Mr. Janssen.

"He's going to be the winner, you know," said Nancy.

"Why, congratulations again, on that, too," said Mr. Janssen as he started up his motor. "I'm proud to know you."

"Thanks," said Nancy.

Well, that worry was over. Plow Boy could race on the twenty-second at the trial races. Now she must train him and train him and see that he kept fit.

So every few days Nancy rode Plow Boy over to Mr. Johnson's scales. He used them for his pigs, but he was proud to have them used by the derby winner.

[33]

"P.B. must not get under 1300 pounds," Nancy told Mr. Johnson.

"No danger. He's a yolly bit more than 1300, I'd say," Mr. Johnson said.

Every time, the scales read the same, 1540 pounds, and Nancy was so relieved.

"I'm just afraid he may lose," she said.

"Now, don't overfeed him, mind you," Mr. Johnson told her. "Overfeed him and he'll yust be logy. Mind that."

So Nancy did not overfeed him and every evening when it was not too hot she raced him on the Afton Road.

Nancy's father told her some tricks about riding. About gripping the horse with her knees to make him do things. And Jens told her that all the jockeys of the Kentucky Derby rode high on the horses' shoulders. They leaned forward, putting their weight over the front legs. Then the horses could pull their hind legs way forward for bigger and faster strides. Nancy practiced it. It was easy, and fun, too. She almost stood up on her knees on Plow Boy's shoulders and leaned over so that her head was beside his.

"That's fun," she cried. "And he does run faster and there I am near his ear to say: 'Oats.' He can't miss it."

When Plow Boy felt her gather herself up that way and heard her say "Oats," he leaped forward as if he were flying through the air. It was so exciting.

[34]

"Oh, I can beat them all!" Nancy laughed. "Just see me beat them all."

If only he would hold his head up all the time. He looked so silly when he dropped it. Nancy whistled shrilly. The horse lifted his head and rolled his ears around toward Nancy.

"Plow Boy, Plow Boy, hold your head in the air like a proud racer. Do I have to whistle at you all the time to keep it up?"

Only when he was racing and excited did Plow Boy hold up his head as a real horse should. What was the matter with him? She wondered if perhaps there might really be something the matter with him. Was he sick? Was that why he dangled his head? Nancy looked him over carefully. Was his nose hot?

"Let me see your teeth."

They looked too yellow. Plow Boy coughed. When he rolled his eyes, the whites that showed looked pink and veiny.

Nancy was scared. She was in a panic. Plow Boy was sick! And the races only five days away. She counted them on the calendar. Yes, five!

"Mom!" she cried. "Plow Boy's sick!"

"Sick?" her mother said. "Why, he can't be sick! Not Plow Boy. He has to win the races."

"Dad!" Nancy moaned. "Plow Boy's sick!"

"Sick?" her fathed asked. "What makes you think so? He looks as fit as usual."

Nancy told him.

"His teeth are awfully yellow and his eyeballs are pink."

"Well, that sounds about normal in a horse. They don't have teeth like pearls and eyeballs like snowballs. Not ever."

Her father was laughing as usual. He always saw jokes in everything.

"Dad!"

Nancy turned to her mother.

"Mom! He's really sick. He can't hold up his head."

"Now, my Pete," Bill said, "his teeth—"

"Are the same color and his eyes too," his father said. "But, Nance," he said, almost choking with laughter, "that would not make him sick, Nance. That's just the way horses are."

"And he coughed," Nancy moaned.

"Because you were choking him when you were looking at his teeth," her father said. "He's all right, Nance."

"Now, Dad," said her mother, "maybe we should have the veterinarian look him over. We can't have him sick, you know. He has to win the race. It's always best to play safe."

[37]

"O.K., Martha," Nancy's father said. "I'll call Dr. Brown. Then Nance won't worry any more." He went to the telephone.

"Yes," he said. "Can you come over and look at a horse of mine? Well, he belongs to my girl. No, we'd better not ride him over. He's due at the races next week and my daughter thinks he's not up to par. Oh, thanks, Doctor, that's good of you. Be seeing you."

In half an hour Dr. Brown came and was taken out to see Plow Boy. The doctor had a mustache that had slipped down to the edge of his lip. Nancy could not keep her eyes away from it as she led him to the barn. Nancy's mother and father and Jens and Bill all went along to hear what the veterinarian had to say.

Dr. Brown did everything a vet does to a sick horse. Everything to find out what if anything was the matter with him. What was he eating, or drinking, or doing?

"Drink when he was too hot?" he asked.

"No," said Nancy.

"Running him when he was too tired?"

"No. We must make him well. He's the winner of the Plug-Horse Derby, you know."

"Oh, have they run it before? Thought this was the first time."

[38]

"Yes, it is, but he's the winner, you see."

The mustache seemed to be jumping about on the edge of his lip, but he did not really smile.

"Oh, I see," he said soberly. "Then we must be sure he is well. Is he eating all right?"

"Yes," said Nancy. "We give him the right amount and he eats every crumb, or grain rather, or blade, or something, or wisp, maybe."

"Sleep well?"

"Oh, I guess so. I never stay up to watch. Should I?"

The vet did some more things that a vet does to find out if a horse is sick. And then he patted him on the neck and rubbed his nose. Plow Boy paid little attention to him. He was reaching around and trying to breathe in some grass. Then he sneezed a good healthy horse sneeze.

Nancy was holding her breath with her clasped hands.

"You know," said Dr. Brown, "I think this is about the healthiest horse I ever examined. He's perfectly sound and perfectly fit. I can't find a thing the matter with him."

"Oh, do you think so?" Nancy gasped. "Really, all right?"

"I never saw a righter horse," said Dr. Brown.

His mustache was really smiling now. "And you know, you're right about his being the derby winner. He is just that. Muscles firm, good tone."

[40]

He shook hands with Nancy and slapped Plow Boy on his black side.

"Good luck, old boy," said the doctor.

"Oh, thanks," said Nancy.

"Such a relief," said Nancy's mother.

"Sure is," said her father, grinning his widest grin.

"Oh, Doctor," Nancy said. She was dragging her purse from her pocket. "I didn't pay. How much is it?"

Dr. Brown was smiling at her.

"But there's nothing the matter with him. I did not do a thing for him."

"You drove all the way over. It took your time."

"Didn't have anything else to do. Proud to meet the derby winner," said Dr. Brown, bowing.

Nancy looked at her father for help.

"Gas," his lips said without speaking.

"But there's your gas," said Nancy. "There's your gas. I could pay for that."

The vet looked at Nancy. Her forehead was wrinkled with worry.

"I have the money," she said. "Right here. I sold the eggs my chickens laid. It's my horse and it's my money."

"Well, all right," said Dr. Brown. "Say fifty cents for the gas. Thank you very much, Miss Nancy. That is good of you. Good luck to the racing."

Dr. Brown climbed into his car and drove away along the lane toward the highway.

Nancy watched him go. She rather liked that mustache after all. At least on Dr. Brown.

"Oh, Doctor, wait a minute," she yelled after the car that was already turning onto the highway toward town. "I forgot," said Nancy. "I just forgot to ask him about his head."

"Ha, ha, ha," laughed Bill. "You can't do anything about his head. Not a head like that. It's just that hanging kind."

Nancy glared at Bill from under her frown as she stuffed the purse into the pocket of her jeans.

Bill was an oaf, she thought!

ON THE WAY

Early in the morning of the twenty-second of August Nancy brushed some dust from Plow Boy's coal-black flank.

"I'll brush you again before the race," she promised him. "You show up every speck of dust, you are so black."

Plow Boy's sides were glimmering even in the gray light of before sunrise. His hoofs wore pale polish too. Nancy had used her own tan shoe polish and buffed them with her own shoe brush. She led him over to the fence and climbed on. Her father was grinning as usual.

[44]

"Believe in an early start, don't you, Nance?" he chuckled.

Her father always saw the funny side of things. And if there was no funny side, he laughed nevertheless, a deep rumbling laugh that made everyone else laugh, too. Nancy giggled now.

"I don't want to be late, Dad. We're supposed to be at the scales at nine o'clock, you know. I'm going to walk him, so he won't be tired for the race, and it's eight miles."

"Even then." Her father laughed.

"Now, Dad," her mother said, "let the girl go early if she wants to. Starting early she won't have to worry about being late. The bird that comes early is never tardy."

"No, she won't have to worry about that. Why, it's all right, Nance," he said. "There's nothing like being at a place on time."

"Here's your bag, Nancy," said her mother. "I've put everything in."

She always remembered things, Nancy's mother did. In the bag was a brush to brush Plow Boy with at the last moment. A clean pair of socks for Nancy so that she would be neat and clean. And sandwiches and apples so she would not be hungry. Her purse with the egg money was tucked into the pocket of her jeans and buttoned up. Fastened to the handle of the sandwich bag was the rope of

Plow Boy's feed bag with his oats. Her father draped them over Plow Boy's neck. They rested safely on each side.

"O.K., Nance," her father said. "We'll follow along in the car soon and be there for the races. Sure you know where the scales are? Next to the Administration Building?"

"Yes, I know, and if I should lose my way, I can ask," Nancy answered.

"Don't forget to eat," her mother warned. "Don't get so excited that you forget to eat."

"No," laughed Nancy. "No danger."

But now that she was about ready to leave for the races, she felt just a little mite scared. Of course Plow Boy was all right and he would win his race, wouldn't he?

"Well, good-by," said Nancy.

"Good-by," everyone called, except Bill. He was too busy polishing up his horse Pete. He was much too busy to notice.

"Bill will be right along after you, Nance," her father said.

As she turned toward the lane to the highway, Nancy felt tinglings going up and down her spine. Tingly tingles going up and down.

"Good-by," she said. "Get going, P.B."

Plow Boy was not at all excited. He jogged along with

[46]

his head thrust forward as he usually did. He walked along the shoulder of the highway.

It was cool and hazy that morning. Cool and dim and mysterious. The farm buildings stood like gray blocks among the gray trees. It was so strange and quiet. Nancy had never before gone riding so early in the morning. The sound of Plow Boy's hoofs was loud in the stillness. His sneeze was like a clap of thunder.

On Nancy rode toward the city, bobbing and swaying with the bounce of Plow Boy's wide back. She passed the yellow fields and the green corn, the corn and the yellow fields. She waved at Jennie Jones who was taking her father's cows to pasture. The gravel on the shoulder crunched under the horse's hoofs. Nancy whistled under her breath. A meadow lark answered from a telephone wire.

"Yo ho, Plow Boy. How are you feeling?" Nancy asked.

Plow Boy answered by turning his ears around in the sockets, then front again in the direction he was going. The sky was a misty, glowing yellow. The sun came up above the trees. It was not red, it was golden.

"It will be a pleasant day, P.B.," Nancy said. "Do you suppose I'm hungry?"

Nancy pulled a big watch from her shirt pocket. Jens had let her borrow his so she could be sure to know what

[48]

time it was. It was pinned fast to her shirt pocket with a large safety pin. She must not lose it.

"Why, it's seven o'clock," she said. "Of course I'm hungry. I had breakfast at five."

Nancy opened the bag and took out one sandwich. Chicken always tasted good and there was lettuce from the garden and her mother's salad dressing. How many were there? Could she have another? Yes, there were a lot of them. Yes, she would. And after that she took another, because she still felt hungry. She ate an apple and half of another apple. She leaned forward over Plow Boy's neck and stuffed the other half between his teeth.

"He loves apples so," said Nancy, as she listened to the loud crunching from the direction of Plow Boy's mouth.

Eight miles was a long distance for walking a horse. Plow Boy was walking eight miles to race one quarter-mile. That seemed rather ridiculous. It was taking two hours about to go to the place where he would run for half a minute. Yes, it was ridiculous if you thought about it that way. Of course, there was the money, if he won this race and the final race on Labor Day—if he did win them.

"But of course you will, P.B.," Nancy told him, so that he would not be worrying about it.

Once Plow Boy stopped to eat some green grass and rest in the shade. Once he drank from a pond with his usual

[49]

loud guzzling. The sun was warm and growing warmer.

"There it is, P.B.," Nancy shouted. "There it is, the city!"

The city was a misty-blue silhouette high against the sky.

"See the tallest building? It's a skyscraper, the bank is."

The bank reached its sign high up in the mistiness. The houses along the street grew closer together. There were half-dozens of them in a block. There were grumbling buses and scores of automobiles going to work.

Plow Boy walked slowly on. It was all the same to him. Meadow larks or skyscrapers were all the same to him. At last they came to the wide avenue that led to the gate of the Fair Grounds. Inside the gate were the Fair buildings, beautiful lawns, and flower beds. The grass was as bright as new green paint.

"To the Administration Building," one sign read.

"Plug-Horse Derby weighing-in," said another, with a large hand pointing.

Nancy rode along the turn of the driveway under the trees. The Fair Grounds looked clean and polished. There were no crowds, no blaring music. The white-towered Agricultural Building all in new paint was across the way. In the distance were the Hippodrome for the livestock shows, and the huge bulk of the grandstand. There were

groups of men here and there hammering some last-min-
ute nails for bunting and flags. Or painting popcorn- and
hot-dog stands. Or putting up tents. And women were
scurrying around with pies and cakes and things in their
arms. The huge, growling farm machineries in their red-
dest paint came plodding in before and after her. People
were all a-bustle to ready things for the Fair opening on
the following day.

"Now over there must be the scales," said Nancy.
"Where the crowd of people is and the horses."

There were boys and girls near the scales and a
few grown-ups. Some of the horses were being held fast
by their owners. Some were still stumbling down from the
trucks and trailers that brought them there.

"We walked, didn't we, P.B.? We did not come in a
truck and we are not a bit tired. Say no."

Plow Boy shook his head as Nancy slid down from his
back. It was half-past eight by Jens's watch.

"Get in line, all of you," a man was shouting. "We'll
start weighing now, there are so many. It doesn't matter
who's first. Come, you first," he said to a redheaded boy
leading a roan horse.

There were several men helping to line up the horses.
And two or three were around the scales doing the weighing. The first horse walked on the scales.

"O.K.," the man in charge said. "Let's see now. What's your name? The rider of this fine roan steed."

"Bob Wilson," said the redheaded boy.

"Wilson, Wilson," said the man, fingering over his cards. "Here it is. Bob Wilson, Maiden Rock?"

"Yes, sir," answered the redheaded boy.

Nancy had never seen a redder head. It was bright carrot with a dash of tomato added and a little paprika and some red pepper. It gleamed in the sun. And the boy's face was as pink as strawberry jam.

"O.K., Bob," said the weighing-in man. "Hold still there. What's his name?"

"Buck," said Bob.

"Hold still, Buck. Don't stamp to make yourself weigh more. There it is, 1430 pounds. O.K., you're O.K. Here he is, Bob. Next."

A skinny boy led a thin-looking horse to the scales.

"Ho, ho," said the man. "They grow lightweights on your farm. Now that horse looks under to me, I'm afraid. Oh, too bad, kid. He's only 1250 pounds, not 1300. Sorry, he just can't run. Too bad. Better luck next time. Feed him up some."

Neither the horse nor the boy said a word. The skinny boy led the lightweight horse off into the crowd. They both looked very unhappy.

[53]

And so it went. Horses brown, bay, dapple, and white: 1400, 1350, 1325 pounds; two under 1300. It was Nancy's turn, and she led Plow Boy to the scales.

"Wow!" said the man. "Now that's a horse. Look at him. Wow! Look at that monstrous horse. What's your name, lady?" he was grinning down at Nancy.

"Nancy Jane Reed," she answered. "His name is Plow Boy."

"And he can plow too, I'll bet. Reed, Reed. Here you are, Reed, Nancy Jane, Windy Hill Farm, County Road E. Come on, Plow Boy."

Nancy gave Plow Boy a push from behind and he clumped onto the scales. His feet made loud hollow bangs as he walked on.

"Whoa," said the man. "Now, let's see. What is it, Ned? Fifteen hundred? Wow, what a lot of horse—1540 pounds! The champeen weigher of the morning. Bet we don't beat that today. O.K., Nancy Jane Reed, lead him off and don't let him shake the scales down. Be at the track at one o'clock sharp."

Nancy was pink in the face and giggling as she led Plow Boy away from the scales.

"Hi, there, Nance," a man's voice called. "How are you and the Boy today?"

"Still planning to win the race?" another voice said.

[54]

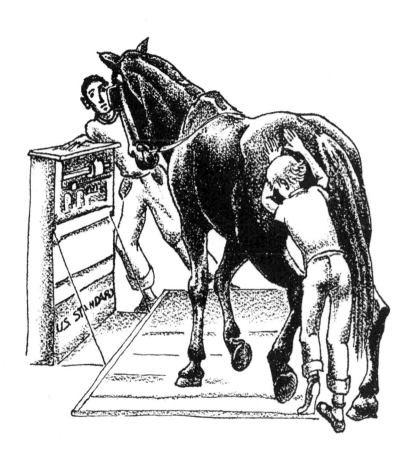

"Why, Johnny," Nancy cried. "And Steve! You here today?"

"Well, of course. Came to write up how you won a race," said Johnny.

"And to take your picture winning it," said Steve.

"Do you see anything of Bill?" Nancy asked. "You're higher up."

She was standing on tiptoe and peering around anxiously.

"Your brother? We never saw him, you know. Here, I'll put you up on the horse so you can see," and Johnny swung her right up on Plow Boy's back without waiting to help her mount. Maybe knights swung their ladies up that way. She hoped so.

"I'm afraid he's late. It's after nine. No, there he is right at the end of the line. Pete looks all right. Sometimes he's a little bit skittish. He does unexpected things. Oh, and there's Mom and Dad on the edge of the crowd. Yoo-hoo!" Nancy called, but they did not hear her. "I'd better go over to them. Maybe I'll see you afterwards."

"You bet," said Johnny, bowing a little. He would have taken off his hat if he had been wearing one.

"Good-by," said Steve.

Nancy rode Plow Boy through the crowd and joined her

mother and father. They walked over to the shade of a huge elm to wait for Bill. It was a hot day. It was hot already at ten o'clock.

"The man liked P.B.," Nancy said.

"How could he help it?" laughed her father. "Great hulk of a horse like that."

"Good thing he can't understand," Nancy said. "Imagine calling him a hulk! That sounds awful."

"He's a beautiful creature," Nancy's mother said in her solemn way. "A beautiful, beautiful creature."

At last Bill came riding over on Pete.

"Man said he is a good horse—1460 pounds. But he acted up so, Pete, I mean, when I tried to march him on the scales. He danced and kicked and tried to turn around. He's a scamp. Do you suppose he'll act up at the races, too?"

Bill's father was patting Pete's neck and Pete was nuzzling him.

"Good boy," said Bill's father. "Good boy. Be sure not to aggravate him, Bill. He's touchy, but he is all right if you are firm and gentle."

"Firm and gentle, how can you be firm and gentle at the same time?" scoffed Bill.

"Oh, yes, you can. Don't be rough, don't jerk or shout

[57]

or kick him with your heels. Don't let him know you are worried. Just hold firm on the reins and speak quietly. You know how, Bill."

"O.K., Dad," Bill said. "I'll sure try."

"Let's go over there under those trees and eat our lunch," Nancy's mother said.

"Yes, and the horses can have some cool grass to refresh them for what's to come," said her father.

They drank their cold lemonade from the thermos jug and ate sandwiches and trimmings. Nancy looked at Jens's watch every few minutes to see whether one o'clock might be coming along.

"Don't rush, Nancy," her mother said. "Just eat your sandwiches."

"O.K., Mom," Nancy answered, as she bit into her sixth one.

THE SECRET WORD

At last it was half-past twelve.

"Well, guess we'd better start," said Nancy's father. "It is a good walk over to the grandstand."

"He said one o'clock sharp," said Nancy.

Nancy was brushing Plow Boy's neck and sides and back. She brushed at his mane and tail. She ran her fingers over the long black hairs of his mane. That was one of his beauties, she thought. He seemed to like it, too. He always seemed to like to toss it so that it flopped on his neck, and it fluttered beautifully when he was running.

"O.K., Nance?" her father asked.

"Oh, sure," Nancy said.

Her father helped her mount Plow Boy. Then she and Bill on their horses strolled over toward the grandstand. There were several horses coming along the roadways from different directions. Nancy saw the redheaded boy leading his roan horse. His hair certainly was red. It looked redder than ever in the noon sun.

At the grandstand the stewards who had helped with the weighing were now sorting the horses. They were putting the horses together in groups, those of similar size in a group.

"Nancy Jane Reed," one of them was calling. "Nancy Jane Reed, 1540 pounds."

Nancy's father snorted with laughter.

"Nancy Jane Reed, 1540 pounds," he repeated.

He was laughing so hard that her mother led him away to their seats in the grandstand where they were to watch the races.

"William McIntire, 1500 pounds."

"Olaf Olson, 1495 po nds. You three will be the fifth race," the man said. "Wait over there in the shade of the grandstand until we call you. Race number 5, remember."

From behind the grandstand Nancy could not see anything that went on. She could hear the men's voices calling and directing. Other horses and jockeys came into the

[60]

shade near them. The two boys in the fifth race were looking Plow Boy over.

"He sure is a big horse," one of the boys said, the one called William.

"But big horses can't run so fast," said the other boy.

"He can run all right," Nancy told them.

"Girls can't ride anyway," William said. "They aren't strong enough."

"You haven't a chance," said Olaf. "Too bad."

Nancy patted Plow Boy's neck and ran her fingers down his mane. She grinned to herself. The boys did not know about the secret word.

"And we won't tell, P.B., will we? That secret word!"

"Are you the only girl in the races?" Olaf asked.

"No, there's another one over there and there's another. Girls can ride."

"Haw," the boys taunted. "Girls can't ride! You show me."

"O.K., I will," Nancy said. "You wait and see. You may get a surprise."

Nancy could see Bill far down the line. Pete was dancing. She wondered what race Bill was in. Two men came along to see that everything was all right and that all the horses were behaving and the jockeys too.

[61]

" 'Twon't be long now," one of them said. "We start in just a minute. Remember your race number."

Then they could hear the shout over the loudspeaker.

"Race number 1. Contestants will bring their horses around to the track. Race number 1!"

The voice sent shivers down Nancy's spine and out into her fingers and toes. It was the beginning. She wished she were in the first race.

"P.B.," she said in his ear. Plow Boy nickered a gentle little nicker. It sounded like: "Don't worry, old girl, we'll do it."

There was the sound of shouting voices and orders, then the thudding of horses' hoofs. In less than a minute it was over. There was shouting and clapping for the winner.

"Race number 2!" the megaphone thundered.

It was coming nearer, Nancy thought. She fiddled with Plow Boy's bridle. She turned around and straightened his tail. She leaned over and looked at his left foot. Why his left foot, she did not know. It had not been bothering him. It was just to be busy.

"Race number 3!" called the megaphone.

"Oh." Nancy groaned to herself.

The two boys who were racing against her were studying Plow Boy again.

"Too bad he's so big and clumsy," William said.

[62]

Nancy smiled so they would not know how scared she was.

"Too bad you're a girl, too," the other boy said. "You're too little for that horse. You'll never manage him. Ole here is just the right size."

He slapped his white horse's neck. "Good old Ole!" he said.

"You're awful little," said William.

"How old are you?" asked Olaf.

"Eleven—going on twelve," Nancy answered.

"Huh! You're just a baby. We're fourteen."

Nancy smiled harder so that they would not know that she was a little cross. That was Bill's age, too, and they were just like Bill. She guessed boys were all alike. Oafs. Just oafs!

"Race number 4!" bellowed the megaphone.

Nancy could not see Bill anywhere. Had he been in one of the races already finished?

"Come on, now," one of the men said. "Get ready. You're next, number 5. Move up to the gate to be ready."

The three horses stepped out of the shade into the hot sunlight and along the road to the gate of the race track. The fourth race horses were pounding their quarter-mile to victory. There were hundreds of people in the grandstand. They were shouting and urging the riders on. Then

[64]

the race was over and the horses loped on around the track.

"Head up, P.B.," Nancy ordered. "Remember the secret word."

"Race number 5!" the megaphone shouted.

At the word *five* the tingles began galloping up and down Nancy as fast as she meant to race Plow Boy. Nancy and the two boys rode up the bank to the track and around to the starting place.

"There you are," said one of the men. "Steady!"

"Nance, Nance!" It was Johnny calling. "Steve's at the finish line waiting for you."

Nancy was too excited to answer.

The man in charge was saying: "When the flag drops, watch the flag. Now, steady, steady. Hold that horse there. *Go!*" and down went the flag.

The horses took off!

Nancy crouched over Plow Boy's neck as he leaped into the lead. He had a good head start, but Nancy could see the white horse creeping up beside her, that white horse Ole.

"Come on, Ole. Come on, Ole!" the boy was shouting. He was hitting at him with a little whip.

Ole darted forward. He was ahead of Plow Boy.

Nancy leaned over and spoke the secret word in Plow Boy's ear.

"Oats, P.B.! Oats, oats!"

Plow Boy lifted his head.

"Oats!" shouted Nancy.

Plow Boy did not see any oats, but he trusted Nancy. He gathered his feet under him and at the turn of the track he plunged ahead of the white horse.

"Oats!" shouted Nancy and Plow Boy doubled his feet up faster and thundered his way over the finish line.

"Ahead by a length!" shouted the official as he swung down the flag. "The big black ahead by a length."

Nancy leaned back and pulled on Plow Boy's reins.

"O.K.," she whispered. "Good boy, good boy, P.B. You did it. You did it. I knew you would."

Plow Boy was blowing big breaths through his nostrils. He whinnied.

"Yes, P.B., we'll go get the oats right now. Dad has the feed bag and he'll meet us at the gate. Good boy!"

"Hi, Nance," yelled Steve, waving his camera. "I got you, Nance. I got you. We're proud of you!"

"Thanks, Steve," squeaked Nancy. Her voice seemed to be stuck.

The megaphone was calling for the sixth race. And there was Johnny waving his notebook and shouting.

"Good for you, Nance. Nancy Jane Reed, the fabulous jockey. It's all down here, Nance. In the paper tomorrow."

[66]

"Thanks, Johnny," Nancy said. Her voice was coming back again.

Would Johnny ask her for her autograph? But he did not. Nancy led the way back. She had won the race! William and Olaf did not have a word to say about too-big horses and too-little girls. They just quietly followed Nancy and Plow Boy from the track.

It was a hot ride back home after Plow Boy had finished his oats and hay and Nancy had devoured two double ice-cream cones. They were both glad to reach home. Plow Boy was rubbed down and so was Pete when he and Bill straggled in. Then the family sat down to supper. It was good and the whole family, including Jens, ate quantities of food.

Nancy was very quiet during supper, even though she was nearly bursting with happiness. She was quiet because Bill had not won his race. She just ate her supper and did not say a word.

"What happened, Bill? Tell us what happened," his father said, and for once he was not laughing.

"It was Pete," Bill said. "Something got into him."

"What did he do, Bill?" Jens asked. "He's really a good horse."

"And what made him do it?" asked Bill's mother.

[68]

"He was contrary all morning. Remember I told you?"

"Yes," his father said.

"He was going all right until we came to the turn. He was running good till we came to the turn!"

"Then what, Bill?"

"And then what did the idiot do?" cried Bill in disgust. "Did he go round the turn like any sane horse? No! No! He went around the turn and then kept right on turning. He ran in a half-circle and jumped over the fence into the center where the grass is. And then he did the other half of the circle and jumped the fence onto the track again and ran the other way. It almost jarred my teeth out. That crazy horse!"

"Bad luck, Bill," said his father.

"Too bad," his mother said.

"He needs a bigger track," said Jens.

"He's an idiot horse," said Bill, grinding his teeth.

"He was excited, maybe," Nancy said. "He wanted to win the race so much that he got mixed up. Sorry, Bill."

"Yes, and that plug horse of yours, he never gets excited. That's a good name for him, Plow Boy. He's just a stodgy plow horse. He just runs and runs. He's too stupid to do anything else."

"Bill!" gasped Nancy.

[69]

"Plow Boy is a good horse, Bill," his father said. "He's a good horse and he's fast. He deserved to win. And Nance is a good rider.

"Tell you what, Bill," said his father, "that Pete is a good jumping horse. We'll have to enter him in the next hurdle race we hear about."

"He could jump the tallest hedge in England," said Jens. "I'll bet he could."

"And I'll bet he could, too," said Bill's father, with his rumbling laugh. "He's a hurdle horse, not just a quarter-mile racer. He was in the wrong race, Bill. Steeplechase for him!"

Bill began to laugh.

"Sure!" and he laughed so hard that he nearly choked on his salad. To think of that dumb horse taking the trouble to jump hurdles when all he needed to do was some fast galloping.

"Train him for the steeplechase, Bill," said Jens.

"Don't know that he needs any more training, Bill," his father said. "He's ready now."

They all laughed, even Bill's mother, all except Nancy. She could hardly keep her laughter in. Her shoulders shook with it. But she thought she really should not laugh out loud when her horse had won and Bill's horse had only jumped fences.

[70]

PLOW BOY'S CARRIAGE

Nancy counted the days before Labor Day. Nine days. Nine days to finish training Plow Boy for the great Plug-Horse Derby on Labor Day afternoon. Really only eight days, because they must take him to the Fair Grounds the day before.

"I'll ride him up Sunday morning early," Nancy said, "before it is too warm. You could come along with the car and bring me home."

"You know what?" said Jens, between bites of ginger-bread. "I was just thinking. Down at Churchill Downs the racers come in beautiful padded trucks and railroad cars. Almost like Pullman parlor cars."

[71]

"But we couldn't get a special train for eight miles," Nancy said. "And besides there isn't any track between here and the Fair Grounds."

"O.K., I know that," Jens said. "I was just remarking how real horses come to the race track. Now, Plow Boy should have a trailer and not be obliged to walk all that way to the Fair. A private trailer. Shouldn't he?"

"Well, sure," Nancy's father said. "We have that old horse trailer out in the barn. Haven't used it since we brought Plow Boy here when I bought him at Clover Dale farm three years ago. By crickety, he will have a trailer."

"It's really P.B.'s own trailer, then," Nancy said.

"Why, sure," said Jens. "That's just what it is. His own trailer."

"We could check it over and be sure that it's strong enough for his present weight. And get some new tires," Nancy's father said.

"And maybe paint it blue," said Nancy. "I like blue best."

"I have a better idea," Jens said.

"What?" asked Nancy.

"Aluminum. We could cover it with aluminum," said Jens, as he crumpled up his paper napkin.

He was so pleased with his idea that his grin was enormous.

[72]

"Or paint it with aluminum paint," said Nancy's father. "That would throw off the heat just as well."

"Sure," said Jens.

"And couldn't we have a big umbrella? One of those bright colored stripey ones to keep the sun off his head and everything?" Nancy said.

"Why, sure," said her father.

"I have a better idea," Jens said.

"What, Jens?" asked Nancy and her father in a duet.

Jens was full of ideas today. But then Jens was the racing expert of the family. Of course he had held some of the horses at Churchill Downs when he was a boy and he knew all about racing.

"A sort of canopy up over the trailer. See? I could fasten it to the sides of the trailer and shut the horse in. Then he wouldn't be so afraid when things go past him."

"Swell idea, Jens," Nancy's father said.

"He would feel funny, wouldn't he, with everything passing by him while he's not running himself!" Nancy laughed.

"We can have a window in front," Jens said, "so he can see where he is going. That'll make him feel easier."

"O.K.," said Nancy's father. "Let's go out and look at the trailer."

The three of them hurried to the barn and rolled out

[73]

the trailer. Nancy's father and Jens shook it this way and that. They climbed up into it and jumped up and down to see how much it wiggled.

"Pretty solid," Nancy's father said.

"Sure is," Jens said. "Right solid it is."

"I can get two secondhand tires, in good condition. It's been standing around on these for years and they were old then. They won't be any good by now."

"And we do need good strong ones to hold up Plow Boy," said Nancy. "Good strong ones."

The trailer had high sides about as high as a horse and a high front. The back was a gate and lower than the sides.

"We'll build up the sides and front more," said Jens, "and cover over the top with a roof to keep off the sun."

"And then paint the whole thing with aluminum paint," Nancy's father said, "to keep it cool inside. It's a swell idea, Jens."

"Oh, it's nothing," Jens said, shrugging his shoulders and swinging out his hands. "Ideas just come to me."

Nancy's mother had come out, after she finished the dishes, to examine the trailer too.

"And I have some old quilts in the attic," she said. "We can hang them on the inside of the sides to make them soft just like padded railroad cars."

[74]

"Oh, sure," cried Nancy. "Then if he jostles around, he won't get scratched or scraped. Oh, that's perfect!"

So they all began to be very busy about getting the trailer ready. All except Bill. He stood around with his hands in his pockets and the corners of his mouth turned down.

"Crackpot idea!" he was mumbling to himself. "All that fuss about an ordinary plug horse. Pooh!"

Then he went off to look over his fishing tackle. He and Jim from the next farm were going fishing on Saturday.

But the others rushed busily around at the trailer job. Jens looked it over carefully and hammered in a few nails to be sure it was secure. He added more boards to the sides so that the roof would be high enough for Plow Boy's head—if he should happen to hold it up on the way to the races. Jens cut an oblong hole for a window in front of Plow Boy's nose and fitted it with a frame that would hold glass. The glass would keep the rain out, if it should chance to rain, or snow—only it wouldn't snow in September, not even in this state. Then he stretched a canvas over the top for a roof.

"It's going to be wonderful, Jens," Nancy said. "Look, P.B. Look at your new carriage." But she could not make Plow Boy look that way.

[76]

Nancy's father drove to town and bought two new old tires at Smith's garage, strong enough ones to carry Plow Boy.

Nancy and her mother climbed up to the attic and brought down the quilts and tacked them up inside the trailer. One was red and the other was a crazy quilt with more colors in it than there are in the rainbow. They tacked them taut and tight on the inside walls. Nancy practiced bumping against them to see whether she could hurt herself.

"They're perfect," she said.

At last the trailer was finished. The aluminum paint gleamed on the sides and on the canvas roof. Jens was so proud, as he gazed at it with his hands in his pockets, that he almost tipped over backward. Even Bill had to say it was handsome.

"But, pooh, a big horse like that should be able to walk that little distance. Eight miles. It's a silly idea."

"We think it's a grand idea," Nancy said, with her nose in the air. "A very wise idea for a race horse."

"Huh!" said Bill. "A race horse! A fancy carriage won't make him a race horse."

"You wait and see," snapped Nancy. "He's going to win. So there!"

[77]

The next thing was to persuade Plow Boy that he wanted to ride in his trailer. Nancy's father had made a ramp of boards with cleats nailed across so that Plow Boy would not slip. He let down the back door of the trailer and leaned the ramp against it. Plow Boy pawed at the ramp with one hoof and snorted. But at last Nancy succeeded in leading him up and into the trailer. She tied the halter fast and her father fastened the gate. Plow Boy whinnied loudly.

Then Nancy's father fastened the trailer to the car and drove slowly around the barnyard. During the following week they were taking Plow Boy for rides on the highway, faster and faster rides to let him get used to riding in his new carriage. Usually Plow Boy was neighing loudly all the way. They did not need to use their automobile horn to let people know they were coming.

"He might really rather get there by himself, but isn't it an elegant carriage!" Nancy said.

Jens thought yes, it was. He was still bursting with pride because it was his idea, his very own idea out of his very own head.

While they were training Plow Boy to ride in his carriage, Nancy continued training Plow Boy for the race. She practiced gathering herself up on his withers and squeezing her knees against his shoulders. When she did that Plow

[78]

Boy would at once leap forward with long strides that carried him as fast as the wind. Then she kept him going by shouting the secret word.

"Oats! Oats!, P.B., oats!" And Plow Boy would gallop faster than ever, even faster than the wind, faster than the wind in a hundred-mile gale.

"Whoa, whoa!" And Nancy would lean back and pull

on the reins to stop him. "Superb, P.B., superb! You are simply superb! What horse could ever beat you?"

Plow Boy would whinny and shake his head from side to side until his bridle rattled, and take off for home. He would jog off for home and the oats as if he had not been racing at all.

"He's wonderful," said Nancy. "Now if only it does not rain on Labor Day."

That was the big worry. It must not rain. Nancy rubbed Plow Boy down until he shone. Jens was watching her. And it was then that Jens had another idea.

"You know what?" he said. "I have another idea."

He was looking up into the sky and he was looking very wise.

"What, Jens? Tell it," Nancy said, giving the last brush to Plow Boy's mane.

"You might not like it," said Jens, holding his fingers pointed together like a church against his mouth.

"What, Jens?" Nancy asked.

She was leaning against Plow Boy and smoothing his beautiful black mane.

"What, Jens?" she asked.

Jens watched her with a big question in his eyes.

"No, you wouldn't like it. I can plainly see you wouldn't like it. Let's forget it."

[80]

"Oh, Jens! But how can I know whether I like it, if you don't tell me?"

Jens shook his head.

"No, it was just an idea I had. It was a sort of race-horse idea. You know how interested I am in racing."

"Yes, Jens."

"Well, I look at the pictures of race horses, all I can find, and do you know what?"

"What, Jens?"

"They're all sort of trimmed up for the races."

"With flowers, you mean?" Nancy asked.

"No. Not trimmed that way, I don't mean. Neated up. Extra things cut off. Trimmed, you know."

"What's cut off?"

"Well, like hairs," said Jens. "You know, haircuts."

Nancy was still stroking the shining mane of race horse Plow Boy.

"Hair?" Nancy said. "You mean they're shaved all over?"

"Well, they're clipped—clipped around the feet and hocks," Jens stammered.

"Oh, sure, then," Nancy said. "Sure. We'd better trim Plow Boy up."

"And—" said Jens.

"And what, Jens?"

"No. You wouldn't like it, Nancy. No. You won't. Forget I said anything."

Nancy stamped her foot.

"Trim what else, Jens? Tell me this minute!"

"His mane, Jens?" asked Nancy's father as he joined them.

"Well, yes," said Jens, watching Nancy out of the corners of his eyes.

"They crop their manes, Nance, to make them, well, smarter looking," her father said.

Nancy's mouth was hanging open. The hair of Plow Boy's mane was still between her fingers.

"It sort of gives them class," Jens said. "The racers do it. It makes them snappy."

"Their manes?" said Nancy.

"It would sort of snap up his neck," Jens said. "Make his neck arch more. It's really good, you know."

"It would look better, by jinks," said Nancy's father. "Yes, I think we should do it. Hey, Nance?"

"His head won't look so droopy, don't you know," mumbled Jens.

"His beautiful mane, that he's so proud of?" Nancy said. "His gorgeous long black mane?"

"No. You don't want to do it," Jens said. "Just forget I ever mentioned it."

[82]

"It would make his neck look better and his head not so dangling?" Nancy asked.

"Well, I thought so, but just forget it," Jens said, his hands in his pockets and teetering up and down on his toes. "It was just an idea."

"Crop off his mane and he'll look twice the winner," said Nancy's father. "Really, Nance. And it will grow out again, you know."

Nancy looked hard at Plow Boy's neck that was, as usual, rather droopy.

"O.K.," she said. "Crop it off while I'm not looking."

But in the end she watched them. She watched because she wanted to know right away how Plow Boy looked. And she must be sure that it was done correctly. She helped them even it.

"A little more here. And here. Yes, yes, yes, Jens," she said. "He does look more like a race horse. It's really very becoming to him. His neck does arch more."

"I'm glad you like it," Jens said, running his fingers through his own wood-shaving hair that could have taken some cropping, too. "He sure looks like a race horse now. He's champing at the bit right now to get to the races."

And only a few days later he did start. On the Sunday before Labor Day, in the afternoon, they started for the

[84]

Fair Grounds. Nancy's father decided that Jens should drive with Nancy, seeing that the whole idea of the trailer was an idea from Jens's own head. So Jens climbed in behind the wheel and felt very important indeed.

"Good-by, good-by!" And off they started, Jens and Nancy in the seat of the Chevrolet and Plow Boy in the whole of the gleaming, aluminum-painted trailer behind.

"We won't drive too fast," Jens said, "so's to be sure he won't be frightened."

They drove along the county roads and into the city with Plow Boy in his carriage following behind. Plow Boy kept neighing loudly and the people kept turning and looking.

"He's as good as a fire-truck siren any day," Jens said. "Listen to him tooting."

"Hasn't he a musical voice?" said Nancy. "A real pretty voice."

The people smiled when they saw the glimmering trailer and heard Plow Boy inside it. And Jens smiled, too, and waved back at them. He was so proud of his invention. And Nancy smiled and waved, too, because the noise Plow Boy was making was so funny. It must seem ridiculous, Nancy thought, to see this whinnying trailer coming along with no sign of a horse except his tail streaming out back over the gate.

[85]

At last they arrived at the Fair Grounds and drove slowly along the curving drives, carefully feeling their way among the people and the cars. There were crowds of people laughing and looking and chewing candy apples and ice-cream drumsticks. The merry-go-round music was blaring and the big farm tractors and machines on Machinery Hill were grunting and roaring. There was such a din that no one noticed the noise that Plow Boy was making. The chimes in the tower of the Agriculture Building were playing: "It's a beautiful morning," and "Daisy, Daisy, give me your answer true."

They drove by the grandstand to the stables beyond it. Some attendants came out with a gangplank for Plow Boy. They untied his halter but Plow Boy would not come out. The gangplank was different from his and he did not like it. He was whinnying and dancing and would not back out.

"Just a minute," Nancy said. "He's excited with the big ride and all. I'll get him. Move over, Plow Boy," she said slapping him on the back. "Move over and let me in."

She crowded into the trailer beside him and took hold of the halter.

"Come on, old boy, come on. We'll go out and get some oats and hay. Back up, back up. That's it. That's right, P.B."

Plow Boy whinnied again and backed out and onto the ramp.

"Straight back. Steady."

A man stood on each side to help steer him down.

"Whew, what a horse," said one of them. "You going to ride him?"

"Yes," Nancy said.

"Going to win?" asked the other man.

"Oh, sure," Nancy said. "He can run. You'll see."

The men laughed and helped lead Plow Boy into the stable and one of the stalls. The man who was to take care of him patted him on the neck.

[88]

"What a beautiful horse, Miss," he said. "He's as fit as they come."

"Oh, thanks," said Nancy.

"He's the winner, isn't he?" the man asked. "He's the winner of the derby?"

"Oh, sure," laughed Nancy. "That's just what he is."

She waited until Plow Boy was very busy with his oats and hay and then she crept away and ran out to the car.

"Oh, Jens, drive away fast," she cried. "I can't bear to leave him. Drive home fast!"

Jens drove away through the crowds. He leaned out over the car door and looked back at the shining trailer. It was handsomer than any other one there. His smile was proud.

"I think it's going to be a fine day tomorrow," Jens said, peering at the sky and making believe that he was looking for rain and not at his trailer.

"There's a cloud, though," said Nancy.

"Just a summer cloud," Jens said. "No rain in it, not a drop. It'll be a fine day. Mark my word."

"I do hope so, Jens. He's never raced in the mud."

"It's called a soft track," said Jens. "He's never run on a soft track. Eh, Nance?"

"Yes, that's it," said Nancy.

"Or a sloppy track," said Jens.

"Yes," said Nancy. "Yes, mud."

THE PLUG-HORSE
DERBY

It was the evening before the race. The quiet was broken only by the clumping and bumping of a jockey going to bed. This sound died away as the songs of the crickets and katydids took over.

Nancy's mother looked at Nancy's father.

"Do you suppose she'll sleep any tonight," she asked, "with that race coming tomorrow?"

"Oh, I guess so," Nancy's father said. "We took her on that long drive after dinner around by the Indian mounds to get her mind off Plow Boy. She seemed rather quiet when she went upstairs. Children usually sleep."

"And that warm milk should help."

"She sure was worried about leaving Plow Boy overnight at the Fair Grounds," her father said.

"But it's a good stable they have, isn't it?" asked Nancy's mother.

"Yes, and the stable man is good, according to Jens, and he took a fancy to Plow Boy."

"Who wouldn't? He's a beautiful horse in his big, black, bulky way."

"He sure is. Glad I got him. He was a good buy."

"If she doesn't win that race!" Nancy's mother said.

"You know what?" said her father. "If she doesn't win that race, that Nance will just try again next year. But I think she'll win."

"She's a good kid," said Nancy's mother.

"Well, guess we'd better go to bed, too. It'll be a day for us, too, tomorrow, as well as for Nance. Do you think you'll sleep, Martha?" Nancy's father teased. "You're as excited as your daughter, I do believe."

"I'd just as soon have it over, to tell the truth."

Nancy's father shouted out a loud laugh.

"Hush, you'll wake Nancy," her mother whispered.

And the next morning was none other than the morning of the great Plug-Horse Derby at the State Fair, winner Nancy Jane Reed.

At least that was the thought of Nancy Jane Reed when she slid out of bed and into her jeans with one jerk. The second jerk was a shirt. The third jerk was with a hair brush on the top of her head. She'd do a real job just before she started.

"What time do we start, Dad?" she shouted, as she catapulted downstairs.

Of course her father was already out running the milking machines. Jens was washing off the car. The winner of the derby should ride in a clean one, he thought. Bill was doing odds and ends. He was good at that.

"You could go and tend to the chickens now, Nancy," her mother said. "By the time you're through we can eat breakfast."

There were several things to do for the chickens to last all day. Feed, water, and this and that. Nancy scurried around as fast as any of the chickens did. They squawked and ran every time she moved.

"What time do we start, Dad?" Nancy repeated as soon as they were seated for breakfast. "I'd like to be early so as to visit P.B. and cheer him up after his being alone so long."

"Ouch," growled Bill. "How silly can girls be!"

"Well, he isn't used to being away from the family so long."

[92]

"Poor little frail thing," scoffed Bill. "All alone for the night!"

"Well," said Nancy. "And I have to exercise him, too, before the race."

"As I was saying," Nancy's father said, only he had not been saying anything. He had not had a chance. "Or as I was about to say, or was I? I think we could start at about nine-thirty."

"Yes," Nancy said. "That will give me time enough to see that my steed is prepared for the parade."

She slid her eyes to the corners to look at Bill, but Bill was busy with his oatmeal.

"The parade is at two before the whole grandstand full of people. I'm going to wear my new red shirt," Nancy said. "It'll be a spot of color on black Plow Boy."

"Oh, boy! How beautiful!" mumbled Bill. "At least they can see you coming."

"And may I say," said Nancy's father, "that I hope you are wearing your shirt-tail tucked in?"

"Should I?" asked Nancy rather surprised.

"Yes," her father said, "you should!"

"Well, O.K.," said Nancy. "If it'll stay in. Do they wear shirts tucked in at the Kentucky Derby, Jens?"

"Didn't see any flapping around," Jens said.

"Well, then, I'll wear mine in," said Nancy.

[93]

"Good," said her father. "Come on, we'll finish our jobs and be ready by nine-thirty sharp. O.K.?"

"O.K.," the family said in a chorus.

So at nine-thirty they were ready, all of them. Nancy's red shirt was tucked tightly into the belt of her jeans. She looked as if she would burst out at any moment, it was so tight. Her shirt pocket bulged with four handkerchiefs and a pocket comb. Her jean pockets were bunchy with her pocketbook of egg money and three pairs of clean socks.

[94]

Her hair was fastened down with two-dozen bobbie pins. Her father choked at the sight of her.

"O.K., Dad?" Nancy asked, turning round and round and trying not to pull out any of the shirt.

"O.K., Nance," her father answered. "Neat as a pin, neat as a pin, Nance," and he had a bad attack of coughing.

Bill was straightening his necktie. It was the only one he had and he had never before been seen wearing it. His hair was stuck down with pomade.

"O.K., Bill," his father said. "You'll do. Very neat and natty. Let's go."

He was still loudly chuckling as they climbed into the car, and winking at Nancy's mother. Those kids! How funny they were! How funny!

It seemed a long time to Nancy, but it was not very many minutes before they arrived at the Fair Grounds. They parked the car just back of the stables, so that Nancy would be near Plow Boy.

"I'll just run along and see how he is," Nancy shouted as she jumped from the car. "Hope he's all right."

"Ouch!" Bill groaned, making believe he felt sick.

"I'll be along," her father called after her.

Nancy ran over to the stable where Plow Boy was.

"P.B.," she called.

A loud neighing almost shattered the walls of the stable.

"He can still talk," Nancy said.

And there was Plow Boy looking more than usually shining.

"Hope that horse wins," the stableman said as he fluffed up Plow Boy's mane. "Sure is a fine horse. He's so strong and well mannered. He should win."

"Well, he is going to win," Nancy declared. "I don't even have to brush him, he is so beautiful. Thanks."

"And such a big horse," said the stableman.

"Yes," said Nancy's father. "He's a good horse. Fifteen hands—not an inch less. And don't tell anyone, but he is going to win the race."

"That I can believe," the man said.

"He's just teasing," Nancy said. "We're all just teasing, but really he can run. He does not like to let any horse get ahead of him."

"I'd be willing to bet on him. I've seen all the horses, you know," the stableman said.

"Thanks," said Nancy. "Now I'll give him some exercise."

They led Plow Boy out of the stable to the big parking lot in back. Nancy's father swung her up on Plow Boy's back and off trotted the future winner of the Plug-Horse Derby to limber up for the race.

[96]

Afterward the family ate lunch from the basket in the trunk of the car. Just standing up and nibbling or sitting on the ground.

"We really should have gone to one of the eating places for a real meal," Nancy's mother said. "This is no way to eat before a race. Eat plenty, Nancy. Good eating keeps a steady nerve."

"I can't seem to swallow," Nancy answered.

"Poor thing!" growled Bill. "She's scared to death."

"And Plow Boy sort of has the jitters," said Nancy.

"He's scared, too," said Bill. "Must be, must be."

"Come on, Bill," his father said. "I have an idea."

Bill scuffed away after his father, with a grin over his shoulder at Nancy.

"Plow Boy'll be all right, Nancy," her mother said. "I'm sure he will."

"I never saw him so excited," Nancy said.

"All the noise and all the people and so many, many horses," said her mother. "No wonder."

"Yes," Nancy said. "All the wild-West horses and the horse-show horses, neighing and stamping."

"He'll be all right," Jens said. "Don't worry, Nancy. He'll be O.K. when he gets to running. He has mettle, Nance, that horse. They're the ones that win races, you know."

"Well, I do hope so," Nancy said.

Nancy's father came in with a sackful of ice-cream cones.

"This'll go down, Nance," he said, as he held out a double one to Nancy. "This'll slip right down easy."

"Oh, thanks, Dad. It does go down, see!"

"Here's yours, Jens, and you go out and entertain Bill. Take him around to visit the cowboys and keep him off Nance's neck. Here are the tickets for the two of you. Get him to the grandstand in time."

"Sure," Jens said. "I'll keep him quiet."

"That Bill," said Nancy's father. "You never can tell about Bill."

"Bill is an oaf!" Nancy said, as she chewed into her ice-cream cone. "An oaf! Capital O, capital A, capital F, oaf!"

The second cone was even better than the first, Nancy thought.

At one o'clock the jockeys were to be on hand in the paddock with their horses all ready. In the different stables the farm horses were tied while their owners groomed them for the race. There was brushing and combing and general straightening. The other girl jockey was neatly laying each lock of hair of her gray horse's mane beside the next. The mane lay in crimpy grayness to match his neck. The horse's name was Sad Sam. He had a sour-looking mouth.

[98]

The lower lip projected and it was trembling with sadness.

Nancy and her father were busy with Plow Boy. The last speck of dust was brushed off. His mane stood up like a crisp, black hedge along his neck.

"He's really handsome," Nancy declared.

Of course her father was laughing.

Nancy's mother had gone to join Bill and Jens in the grandstand. She wanted to see that race won with her very own eyes.

"Seeing is believing," she said solemnly.

"All right there?" a voice called in the door of the stable. It was the promotion man of the *Pioneer Express.* "Hi, Nancy. Come out now and we'll get ready for the race. Right out back of the paddock."

"I'll keep an eye on Plow Boy," Nancy's father said.

"Is my shirt-tail all right, Dad?"

"Yes, Nance," he said. "You might give it an extra tuck just before you take off. After you're mounted, you know."

"Oh, I have to change my socks."

Nancy leaned up against her father and took off a shoe and changed the sock on one foot and then the other. The soiled pair she put in the pocket with the egg money.

"Better hurry," said her father.

"How about my hair?" asked Nancy.

"Looks all right to me as far as I can tell about such things. These two pins are a mite too close together. There, that's better."

"Thanks, Dad. You're a great comfort to me," said Nancy.

"Yes?" said her father.

"Yes," she answered.

"Now then. Ready to go? I'll come along with P.B.," and they walked out into the sunshine.

"Nance, Nance!" It was Johnny. "Steve's here, Nance."

"Take your picture, Nance? Get up on your horse. Jeepers, how gay you are. I've got my color one here, too," Steve called.

Nancy just laughed. She was too excited to say a word. Steve snapped her this way and that. She looked small and bright on Plow Boy's blackness.

"How are you feeling, Nance? Not scared?" Johnny said. He was making notes in his chunky little notebook. "You look swell, just swell. I'm glad you're going to win."

"Oh, do you think so?" Nancy laughed.

"That's what you told me, isn't it? Sure you'll win."

Was he going to ask her for her autograph? But he did not. Nancy slid from Plow Boy's back.

"I'd better find the promotion man," she said.

"Nance," Johnny was calling after her. "Steve is going

[100]

to be at the finish line and I'll be there, too. Wait for us. Don't rush off."

"O.K.," called Nancy. "I'll be sure to wait," and she ran around some parked cars to find the promotion man.

He was sitting on a box and talking to the boys and the other girl. And, why, yes, there was the redheaded boy! He was holding his roan horse, and they both looked like racers. His head was redder than ever, even redder than her own shirt. Nancy came up to the edge of the crowd. Some of the boys were big and tall, almost like men. Even the other girl was bigger than Nancy was.

"They'll make a good picture on the track," the promotion man was saying, holding out some brightly colored, satiny-looking jockey coats. "Here, this should be big enough for you."

The giant standing next to Nancy took the bright-orange jacket and a cap to match. The boys were looking at them critically and grumbling to themselves.

"They won't be a perfect fit. Here's a green one for you," the promotion man was saying to the redheaded boy. "Put 'em on and see how they go."

Nancy was astonished. The coats had long sleeves and came down below the waist. The caps had sort of puffed crowns and big visors. They would cover people all up.

"Here's one for you," the man said to Nancy. "We figured you'd need a little one. It's the littlest we could find."

Nancy took the pinkish jacket and poked herself into it. It entirely covered her new red shirt. Too bad. She turned the sleeves way back so that she would have hands to hold the reins with. She put the visor of the cap over her neck, so that she could see where she was going.

"And here are your numbers," the promotion man said. "The number corresponds with the number of the race you were in at the try-out races."

"Number one," said the giant in the orange coat.

"Number three," said the redheaded boy. He had his cap tucked under his arm.

"Number five," said Nancy. The other girl was number four.

The huge, white squares with the black numbers on them covered most of the front and the back of the jackets.

"Who's this?" said Nancy's father. "Is this pink-coated creature my daughter Nancy?"

"Oh, Dad, help me pin them on. Here are the safety pins. I feel all swallowed up in this coat!"

"They'll look gay on the track," said the promotion man.

So, while Nancy held fast to Plow Boy her father pinned the four corners of the white squares rather crookedly.

[103]

"There, that's the best I can do," he said at last. "Are you really inside that coat, Nance?"

"All ready?" shouted the promotion man. "Now we'll draw for position from the pole. The one who draws number one is at the pole and has the inside of the track. Jack here'll hold the hat while you draw. Shake it up, Jack, and turn all the numbers down. All right. Draw."

The bright-coated jockeys marched past the hat and each pulled out a card.

"Now," said the promotion man, "which one of you has number one?

Nancy held up her card.

"Number one," she said.

"Lucky girl," the man said. "You'll run the shortest race."

"Number two," said the giant.

"Number three," said the other girl.

"Number six," said the redheaded boy, and so on.

"O.K. It's about time to line up for the parade. Go by the numbers on your jackets."

They all straightened their jackets and jerked their caps and climbed up on their horses. Nancy's father swung her up on Plow Boy.

"Line up by the numbers on your jackets, one, two, three."

[104]

They wheeled their horses into line. The veterinarian in charge of the horses, Superintendent of Horses of the State Fair, rode up on his beautiful palomino and led off the march. He wore a bright red coat around his round stomach, a black cap, white riding breeches, and black boots. He was very handsome.

"Follow me!" he called.

Most of the horses had someone leading them to keep them going along in order. Nancy's father held fast to Plow Boy's bridle. Plow Boy was very much excited and he skipped along lifting his feet high.

"Steady there, Plow Boy, steady there." Plow Boy was trying to go in circles. "Steady, Boy, steady!"

"Give you a hand?" asked one of the attendants near by.

"Thanks," Nancy's father said. "He's restive today."

The man held Plow Boy's bridle on the other side and Plow Boy danced along between them.

"Whoa there P.B.," Nancy was saying. "Steady, steady." But Plow Boy danced on.

"He must be going to win the race," the man said.

The procession walked up the little hill to the grandstand track.

"Here they come!" shouted the loudspeaker.

The thousands of people in the grandstand began to

cheer. The cheer swelled and swelled, shoutings and yells, until it almost knocked Nancy from her horse. The band began to play. Along came the doctor on his prancing palomino. Chico was keeping time to the music. And the giant in his orange coat, and number two, and number three, the redheaded boy without his cap. Number four, Sad Sam, and Nancy, number five. Nancy sitting in jockey fashion, leaning forward with her knees drawn far up on Plow Boy's shoulders. As each one passed the judge's box the announcer called out the name of the jockey and of the horse. Slowly they jiggled past.

Then the horses went on alone without the leaders, to form a dancing line just beyond. Plow Boy kept turning in circles. Nancy looked very small on his huge back. It seemed as if just a jacket and cap were riding him. The line was almost straight, all ten horses pranced slowly forward toward the red flag, slowly forward.

Nancy patted Plow Boy's neck.

"Steady, old boy," she said. "Don't get excited. Keep calm."

Or was it Nancy who was excited?

WHO WINS?

Ten little and big jockeys all wanting to win the race. Riding ten plug horses parading around to the post. Ten plug horses prancing toward the red flag.

"When the red flag drops, the race starts," yelled the loudspeaker. "Watch the red flag!"

They were to race a quarter-mile to the finish line in front of the grandstand. Some of the horses were skittish. Some of the riders looked skittish, too.

Plow Boy, number five, with Nancy Jane Reed up, was stepping along as a race horse should when he was going to win a race, stepping high and jiggling as he went. He looked very fit and his blackness shone in the sunlight. He even held up his head. The tingles were racing up and down Nancy's back and out into her fingers and toes. Her mouth was so dry that her tongue felt stiff.

"Well, you won the other race, didn't you?" she said severely to herself or to P.B. "What are you so scared about?"

The ten horses were dancing along to the red flag.

"Almost there!" shouted the loudspeaker.

Then suddenly four of the horses began running, first one and then three others. Nancy jumped. Had the race begun without her?

"Oh, dear!"

"Not yet," one of the men cried out.

"Come back!"

"Whoa!" he yelled.

"Something seems to be the matter," the loudspeaker said. "Whoa there!"

But the horses ran on, wildly galloping. They crossed the finish line in one dash, a white horse in the lead. The people in the grandstand were shouting and laughing. The jockey on the white horse thought he had won the race. He pulled up his horse and bowed to the crowd.

"Run along back," one of the officials told the four

[108]

riders. "Run along back and get into the real race. You got off too soon."

The boys looked very silly and rode back to the others. At last they were all ready for the start. Ten horses were jiggling on their forty feet, wanting to take off.

"When the red flag drops, that's the time to run," the starter said. "All ready now. Ready?"

Down went the flag!

"They're off!" bellowed the loudspeaker.

Ten riders urged their horses forward. Nancy crouched way over on Plow Boy's withers with her knees clutching his shoulders. Plow Boy pitched himself forward and in three strides he leaped out in the lead.

"Oats, oats!" Nancy called into his ear.

Plow Boy was running for oats and when Plow Boy was after oats no Kentucky Derby runner could run faster.

"Oats!"

Any horse race makes a clattering of hoof beats. But a race of Plug-Horse Derby runners makes a noise no less than two thunderstorms coming over a hill.

"In front by a length, number 5 leads by a length. The black horse Plow Boy leads by a length. Two horses together fighting for second place, number 8 and number 3. Number 3 out in front for second. Buck second by half a length. Plow Boy still leads. Buck gaining on Plow Boy, Buck gaining on Plow Boy. Coming alongside Plow Boy, inside on the turn. It's Buck in the lead, Buck in the lead by a head. Buck by a head!"

From the corner of her eye, Nancy saw the flash of a red head!

"Oh, no!"

"Oats!" she shouted with her mouth close to Plow Boy's ear. "Run, P.B.! Oats! Oats! *Oats!* OATS!" Nancy shouted.

She could feel Plow Boy leaping beneath her. She could hear his hard breathing.

"Oats! OATS! P.B.!" Where was the redhead?

There was the finish flag right in front of her. Nancy shut her eyes. She did not want to see that redhead win. She held her breath and squeezed her eyes tight shut. She had stopped saying "oats."

Neck and neck. Then one horse dropped his head down. The race was over!

"Photo-finish. Photo-finish!" somebody yelled.

"No, the black!"

"No, the roan!"

"The black!"

"The black!"

"Photo-finish!"

[110]

The crowd was yelling: "Who, who, which?"

Steve was galloping off to develop his film. He was the official photographer for the *Pioneer Express.* Two or three other photographers followed him.

"Not official yet. Nothing official yet. Wait for the report," blared the megaphone.

The waiting crowd was still.

"I think it was the black."

"No, the roan had passed him."

The jockeys on their horses were waiting, too. They were waiting where they had stopped beyond the judge's stand. Nancy was stroking Plow Boy's neck. He was blowing big breaths from his widened nostrils. His feet were jittering. The redheaded boy on his roan was near. And Sad Sam looked sadder than ever.

"There, there, P.B. Quiet down. You'll know in a minute who won the race." Her own heart was pounding like a racer's feet, bang, bang, bang!

At last Steve came running up to the judge's stand. They looked at the film.

"The black by a nose!"

There was Plow Boy with his head down and forward. He had dropped his head at the last minute. Plow Boy's nose was the first to cross the finish line!

"The black is the winner. Number five, Plow Boy, rid-

[112]

den by Nancy Jane Reed, is the winner. Time: 28.4 seconds. Plow Boy with Nancy Jane Reed up wins the first running of the Plug-Horse Derby!"

Nancy could not move or smile or even breathe. The crowd broke into wild cheering. It began with a sort of yell that sounded like: "Nance" in Bill's voice. She must be hearing things. Then Johnny was on one side of her and her father on the other. Her father's arm was around her and Johnny was shaking her hand.

"Nance, Nance, congratulations!"

"Good girl. We knew. We knew it! We won, Nance. Didn't you hear? We won, Nance!"

The loudspeaker was still blaring.

"Plow Boy with Nancy Jane Reed up wins the first running of the Plug-Horse Derby. Official time: 28.4 seconds for the quarter-mile. Buck with Bob Wilson up in second place. Sad Sam with Patricia Brown up in third."

"Come over to the stand," an official was saying. "Come over for the presentation of the award."

Nancy began to breathe again. She had to do something. The official was to lead her over to the judge's stand. Nancy slid down from Plow Boy's back. Her legs seemed rather papery.She felt of her shirt but the jockey coat covered it. She felt of her head. The cap had blown away. Her hair was tossed about and most of the pins were gone.

[113]

"Dad, my hair!"

"It's all right, Nance. You look all right. You must have been a shower of bobbie pins during that dash." Her father was shaking with laughter.

Then the official led them away to the judge's stand where they stopped before the promotion man. He was grinning a wide grin as he looked down at Nancy. His eyes were crinkled blue.

"Nancy Jane Reed?" he said.

"Yes," piped Nancy. Her voice was about as big as the squeak of a mouse.

"And Plow Boy," he continued.

Plow Boy heard his name and nickered. How about those oats?

"As you are the winner of the Plug-Horse Derby, Nancy Jane Reed, I have the honor of presenting to you this trophy from the *Pioneer Express*. Congratulations."

He pushed toward Nancy a glittering gold thing.

"Miss Nancy Jane Reed," the promotion man repeated, still holding out the golden trophy toward her.

"Oh," Nancy gasped, reaching out for the trophy. "Thanks. Thank you very much."

She held it fast against her stomach. It was big and heavy.

[114]

"You are a good rider and Plow Boy is a good horse."
Plow Boy heard his name and nickered again.

"He really won the race," Nancy said. "Thank you."

There was Plow Boy whinnying for oats. And Plow Boy pushing against the microphone and almost tipping it over and Plow Boy pushing against the promotion man and almost tipping him over, too. Plow Boy wanted his oats. He meant to have them.

"Be still, P.B." He was sniffing at the golden trophy. "Quiet."

"Quiet," said Nancy's father. "Quiet, Plow Boy." He was holding fast to his bridle.

Steve had been taking her picture and Johnny was writing notes in his plump little notebook. She felt like a movie star. Or even the winner of the Kentucky Derby. Photographers were standing around her taking her picture, a dozen of them. Then Johnny slid another little book between her fingers and a fountain pen.

"Have your autograph, lady? Please, your autograph," begged Johnny.

He was asking for her autograph! At last, he was asking for her autograph!

Nancy took the book and the pen and in round letters that were not too very much shaky, she wrote: "Nancy Jane Reed for my friend Johnny." It was her autograph!

At that moment a very tall bareheaded man came up to Nancy. He was holding a black sort of telephone thing in front of his mouth, and there was a long thick wire

[116]

stretching out in the direction from which he had come.

"Now, we'll get the winner to say a word," he was exclaiming into his mike. "Good afternoon," he said to Nancy. "You are Nancy Jane Reed? And this is your horse Plow Boy?"

"Why, yes," Nancy answered into the thing he was holding in front of her mouth.

"A little louder."

"Yes," said Nancy again.

"Well, you look like a very small person to ride such a big horse. How old are you?"

"Eleven, going on twelve," Nancy answered.

"And how much do you weigh, for instance?"

"Oh, about seventy-five pounds," said Nancy.

Wasn't he funny, she thought. He looked so silly talking and smiling into the black thing and then holding it out for her while she answered.

"And how big is he—Plow Boy, I mean?" the man asked. "He looks as if he could plow a deep furrow." He laughed hard at his own joke.

"Fifteen hundred and forty pounds."

"Listen to that," the man said. "Seventy-five pounds rides 1540 pounds to win the race. The little girl shows the big boys the shortest way round. How does it feel to win a race, Nancy?"

[117]

"Oh, it feels good," Nancy said.

"Well, thanks," said the man. He was wearing the same grin that he had begun with. "Radio audience, that was Nancy Jane Reed who rode her horse in first at the Plug-Horse Derby at the State Fair Grounds. Nancy Jane Reed of Windy Hill Farm in this county. Thanks, Nancy."

Nancy looked after him as he went off, trailing his cord behind him like an endless tail. She had talked over the radio! Over the radio to thousands of people. Wasn't it wonderful! What an adventure! She had been on the air!

Plow Boy was looking impatiently over his shoulder and goggling his eyes at Nancy. He whinnied a loud commanding whinny.

"Oh, thank you," she said to the promotion man. "I must go and give Plow Boy the oats I promised him. It was the oats that made him win the race. Good-by."

They were all laughing and clapping as Plow Boy and Nancy and her father went off along the track toward the gate and the stable. Her father was leading Plow Boy. Nancy was bending backward as she carried the trophy in front of her on her stomach.

"Didn't I tell you?" the stableman said as he led Plow Boy to his stall. "Congratulations. A thousand congratulations!"

"Oh, thanks," said Nancy. "Thanks."

[118]

And there was her mother who had come racing down from the grandstand. She was laughing all over herself.

"The best horse always wins," she said. "I'm so proud of you, Nancy." She was trying to hug Nancy around the golden trophy.

And Jens was trying to shake her hand and saying: "Good as a Kentucky Derby any day."

And there too was Bill waiting to see her. His mouth was stretched in a wide, silly grin. He was standing there

[119]

awkwardly running his hands in and out of his pockets, in and out of his pockets. There the two of them stood keeping the silence between them.

"Glad you won, Nance," gulped Bill at last.

He looked as if his necktie was choking him.

"Why, thanks, Bill," Nancy stammered.

"You rode like a boy," said Bill, scuffing at the dirt of the stable floor. "You sure rode like a real jockey."

"Why, Bill, thank you!" gasped Nancy.

[120]

"Well, I'd better go back to the stand for the auto races," he muttered.

"Thanks for coming, Bill."

Nancy stared after Bill as he turned away. Bill, why Bill wasn't so oafy after all.

"Hey, Nance," Bill called over his shoulder, "your jacket's too big for you!

"It looked ridiculous flapping away there," he called over the other shoulder.

That Bill! You just couldn't tell about Bill!

Nancy had set the trophy on a box outside P.B.'s stall. She reached up and put her arms around Plow Boy's neck.

"Thanks, Plow Boy, for winning the race. It has been wonderful! Johnny asked for my autograph and I talked on the radio. Over the radio, P.B.! To thousands of people, maybe millions! Are you listening, P.B.?"

Plow Boy nickered as he loudly chewed his oats and hay.

It sounded like: "Fine, old girl, but don't bother me now!"

A NOTE ON THE

Type

IN WHICH THIS BOOK IS SET

THE TEXT *of this book has been set on the Fotosetter in a type face named Bulmer. This distinguished letter is a replica of a type, long famous in the history of English printing, that was designed and cut by William Martin about 1790 for William Bulmer of the Shakespeare Press. In design, it is all but a modern face, with vertical stress, sharp differentiation between the thick and thin strokes, and nearly flat serifs. The decorative italic shows the influence of Baskerville, whose pupil Martin was.*